ADVENTUI ANTARCTICA

by
Susan Aguilo

Illustrations by
Mike Motz

GREENLAND

CANADA

UNITED STATES

SOUTH AMERICA

RUSSIA
EUROPE
CHINA
INDIA
AFRICA
AUSTRALIA
ANTARCTICA

To my parents,
for giving me the freedom to shine
and the support to succeed.

Alex and his friends loved going to the local fair. They would go on rides and scream in the haunted house. They laughed through the house of mirrors, and when they climbed the rock wall, Alex always made it to the top first. It was so much fun!

After coming inside, having his shower, and brushing his teeth, it was time for bed. Even though he hated going to sleep, he loved this time of the day because his mom would tell him amazing stories where he was the adventurer.

Alex's mom came in the room, lay down on the bed, and started her tale. Tonight it was the story of "Adventure in Antarctica."

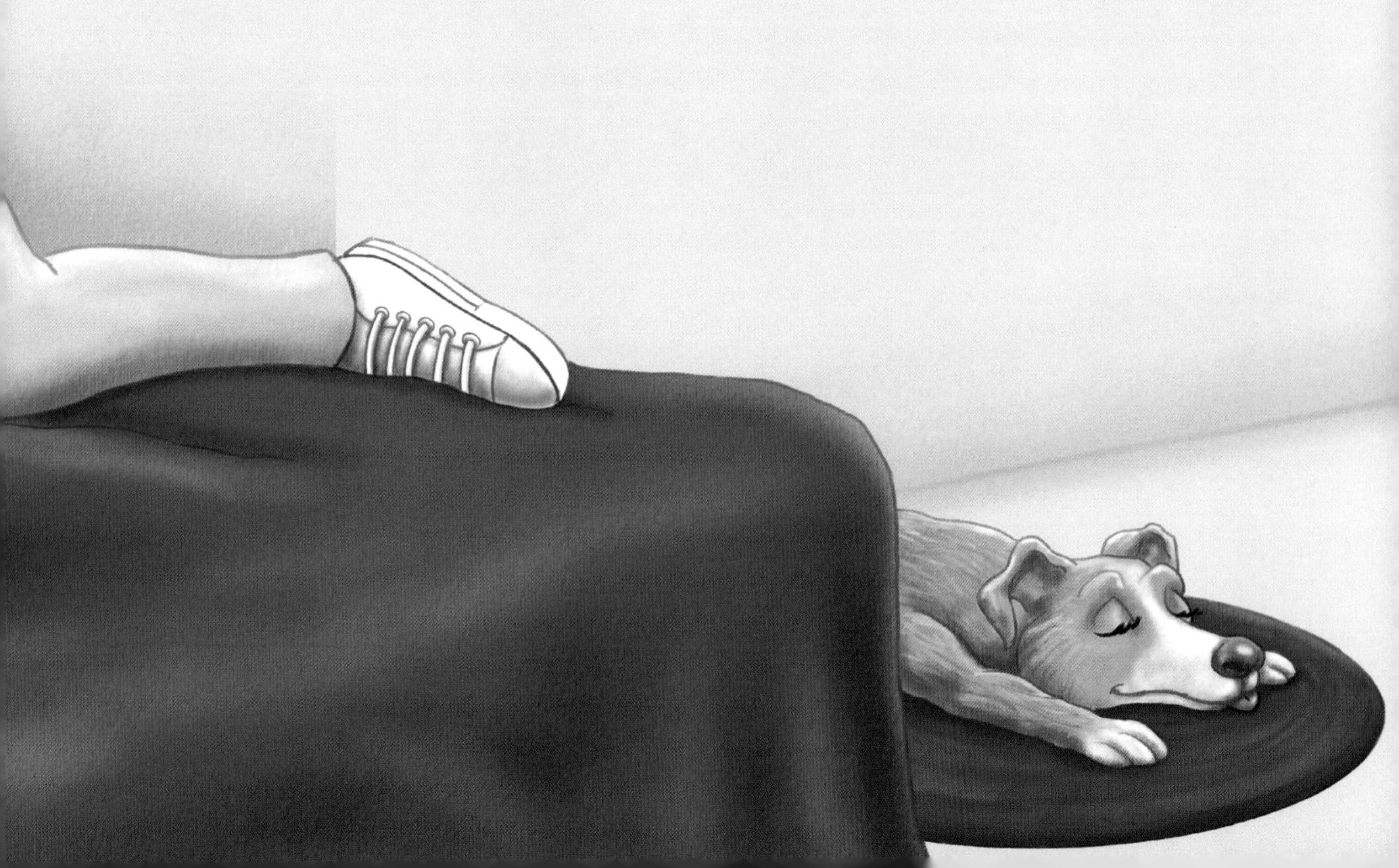

Alex was so excited he could hardly sit still at school. He was going on a two-week polar exploration in Antarctica! His cousin, Victoria, and best friend (and dog), Elmo, would be coming too. Everything was packed and ready to go.

Alex knew he was about to begin the adventure of a lifetime!

Arriving on Antarctica, Alex yelled, “YEAH!” into the wind, punching the air high above his head. Victoria rolled her eyes.

They were shuttled to the helicopter where they would fly to the Antarctic Explorer ship *Vulcan* to spend the next ten days.

Victoria sat up front, taking pictures, while Alex sat in the back, laughing at Elmo, who was wearing an oversized pair of headphones and aviator glasses.

After finding their cabins and dropping their bags, they found their way up on deck. They checked out the humpback whales swimming alongside of the ship before Alex began dragging Victoria up to the front. He had caught sight of a family of Orcas as they passed the bow of the boat. They laughed as the whales jumped and splashed!

That evening they joined a group to watch the aurora lights.

Bright pinks, greens, and blues danced among the stars.
Everyone oohed and awed with delight as the sky was alive with colour!

The next day they took a trip onto land. They saw emperor penguins and the southern elephant seal. It was cold but well worth the trip. The animals were so much cooler to see up close, and they took lots of pictures.

Alex waddled around with his arms down, mimicking the penguins. One of the penguins even smacked Victoria in the forehead, causing Alex to laugh! When Elmo got too close, one of the big elephant bulls chased him away. It was too funny!

They all fell into bed that night *exhausted.*

In the morning, their group took a boat trip around the glaciers to explore.

As they entered one of the bays, a giant chunk of ice fell. It landed in the water with a big SPLASH causing the small boat to bounce and tip. Elmo barked while Victoria grabbed hold of Alex.

After the wave had finally passed, they noticed an underwater cave.
It peeked out of the water like a dark spot on the ice.

Victoria pointed and waved towards a dark shadow in the water as
it bumped the boat.   Something large was moving below!

The large mass turned and looked like it might come back. Scared, the driver of the small boat turned them around, and they sped back to the ship as fast as they could.

Victoria, shaken by the encounter, asked, "*What was that thing?*"

Everyone shrugged their shoulders.

Just as they arrived at the ship, they saw a long tentacle. It slid from the water and wrapped around the zodiac. It pulled the raft down into the water just as Alex stepped off. The group was screaming and running. They now knew what had come from the underwater cave: A GIANT SQUID!

The squid wrapped each of its tentacles around the boat,
trying to grab people as they ran.

Alex, Victoria, and Elmo sprinted by, missing one of the suctioned arms by mere inches. It hit the side of the boat, leaving a dent.

Alex could hear the groaning of the big ship as the giant squid began to squeeze in frustration. He stumbled as he realized the squid was trying to sink the boat.

Alex grabbed Victoria and dragged her to the small submarine on deck. "I have a plan!" he yelled through all the noise. "We are going to use the sub to lead the squid away."

The creature's giant eye blinked as they jumped into the mini sub. It reached out to snatch them just as Alex hit the release button. The submersible dropped safely into the water.

The squid let go of its hold on the ship and slipped into the water, trying to catch the fast moving submarine. The plan was working!

Alex drove while Victoria took some pictures. Her eyes went wide as she watched the tentacles reaching towards them. Elmo was barking with a mixture of fear and excitement.

As they flew through the water, Victoria realized the squid was gaining on them. She screamed, “Faster! We need to go fast, this is not good....not good at all!” She pointed to the cave. “Maybe we can lose it in there.”

Alex turned the mini sub towards the small cave opening. Their only chance was to get inside and hope the cave would protect them. Alex was optimistic that it wasn’t a shallow cave and they wouldn’t be crushed like a pop can. They entered the cave at full speed screaming, “AHHHHHHH!”

As the squid followed them into the tight cave, it hit the sides and ice began to fall. Giant chunks of ice rained down everywhere. One big hunk came down pinning it to the bottom of the cave. More ice fell until the creature had nowhere to go. It was caged in ice!

Alex slowed the submarine to a crawl, avoiding the falling ice.

The tunnel was much deeper than they had thought. They must have travelled for almost a mile under the ice before Alex and Victoria jumped when a voice spoke over the radio. It was the captain of the ship. "Mini Sub, are you okay?"

While Alex relayed their near miss, Victoria drove the submarine. They hoped they could find another exit from this underwater cavern.

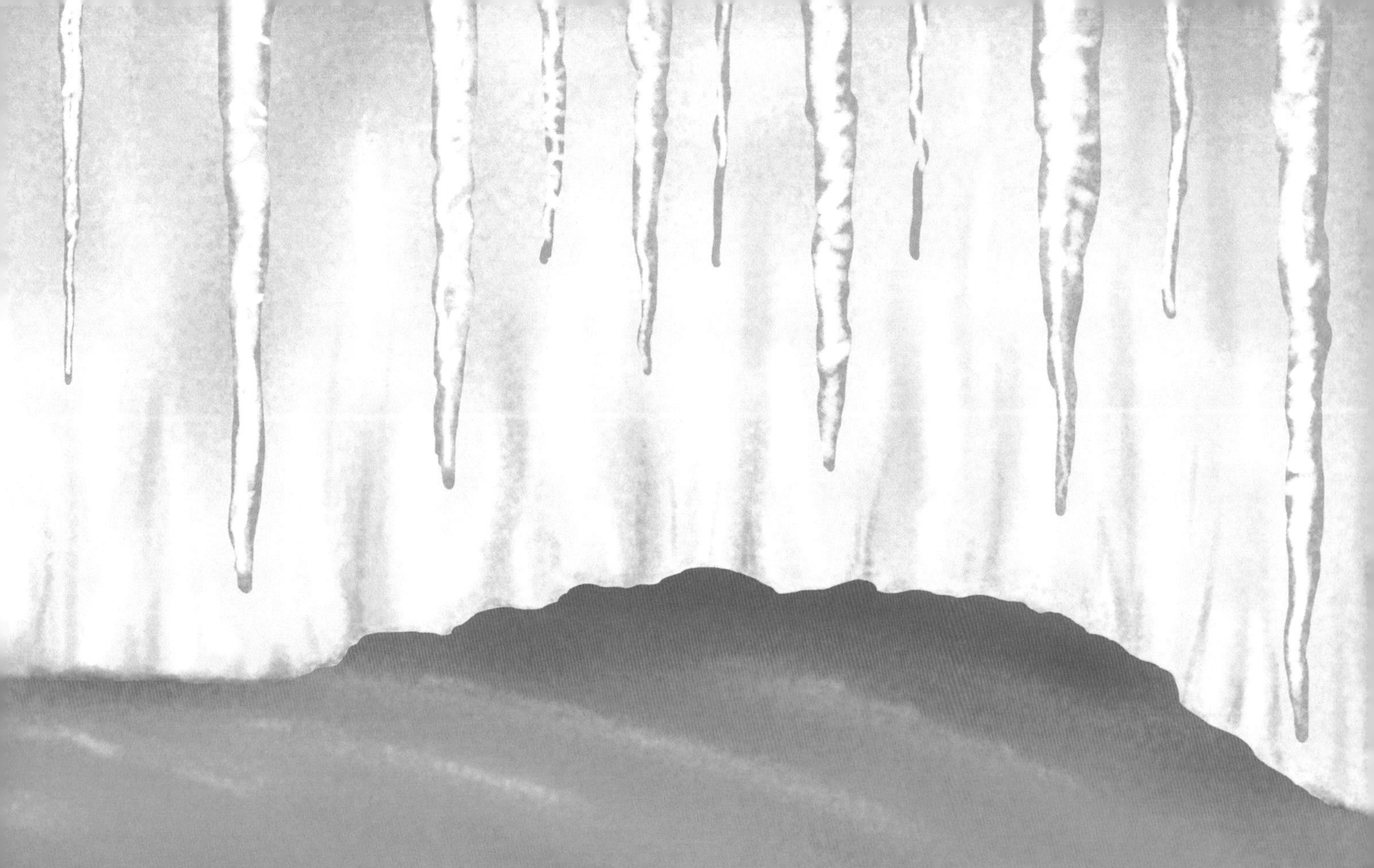

Victoria had been listening so closely to Alex's story that she missed the tunnel's end and the submarine slammed into an ice wall. The sub shook with the impact, and a small crack started along the front glass.

Victoria's eyes widened, and under her breath she said, "Oops!!!!"

Alex looked over, rolled his eyes, and sighed. Taking over the controls, he broached the submarine and found an icy beach. After docking the submarine safely, they looked around and saw that the tunnel continued above the water. They all piled out, climbing their way along the slippery ice cave.

They had only traveled a short distance when the ice tunnel opened up into a large cavern. They just stared. It was unbelievable! The cave was huge, and right in the middle sat a frozen city made of statues, pyramids, and buildings.

The city was shaded in blue light from the ice ceiling above them. It was the most amazing sight Alex or Victoria had ever seen.

Ἀτλαντὶς
νῆσος

Alex, Victoria, and Elmo climbed down from their small cave entrance. They wandered the long forgotten city. Weaving their way through narrow streets, they looked into houses and checked out the statues.

When they finally entered the centre, it was clear to them where they were. They had found the lost City of Atlantis, buried deep under a layer of ice and snow.

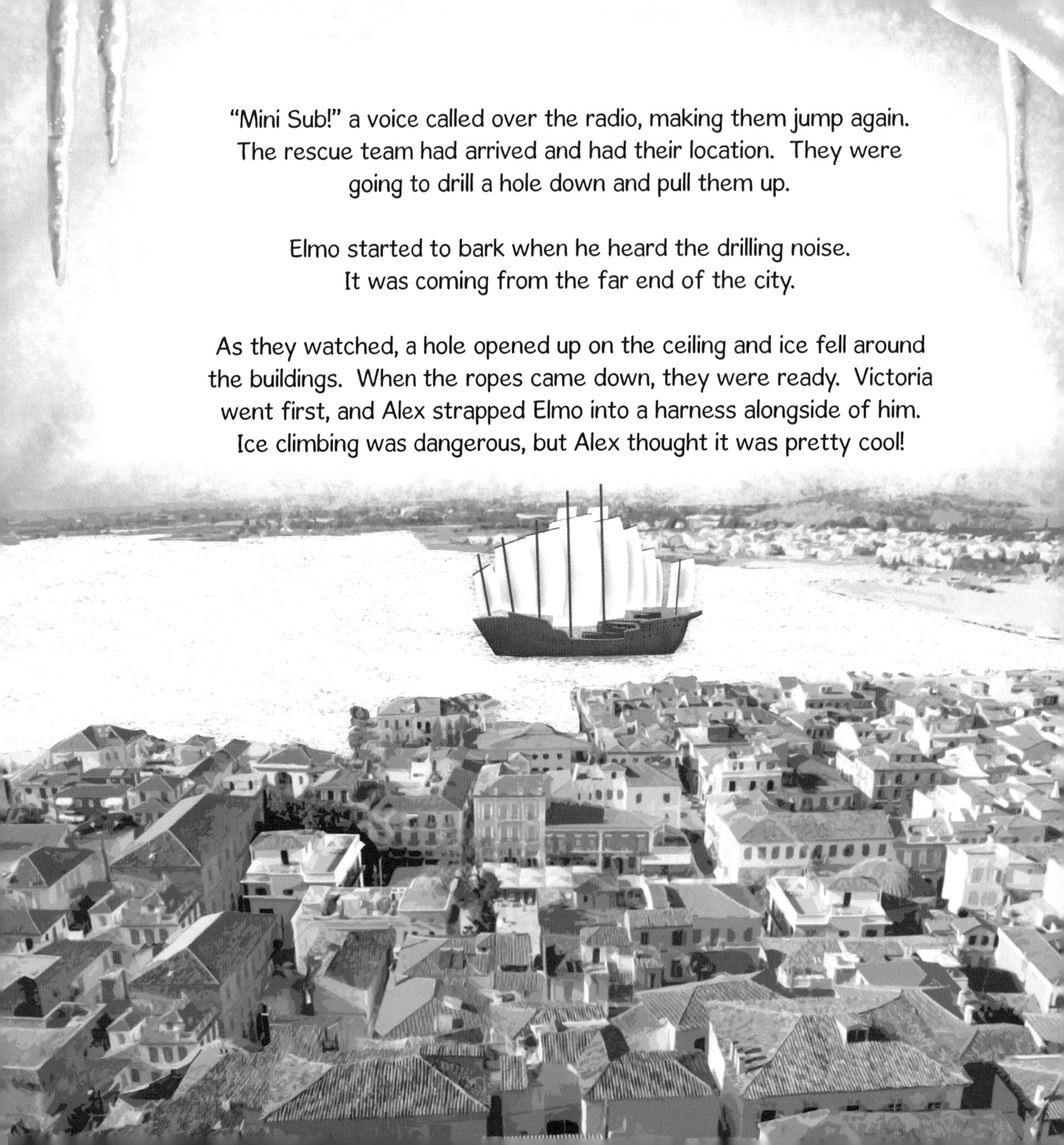

"Mini Sub!" a voice called over the radio, making them jump again. The rescue team had arrived and had their location. They were going to drill a hole down and pull them up.

Elmo started to bark when he heard the drilling noise. It was coming from the far end of the city.

As they watched, a hole opened up on the ceiling and ice fell around the buildings. When the ropes came down, they were ready. Victoria went first, and Alex strapped Elmo into a harness alongside of him. Ice climbing was dangerous, but Alex thought it was pretty cool!

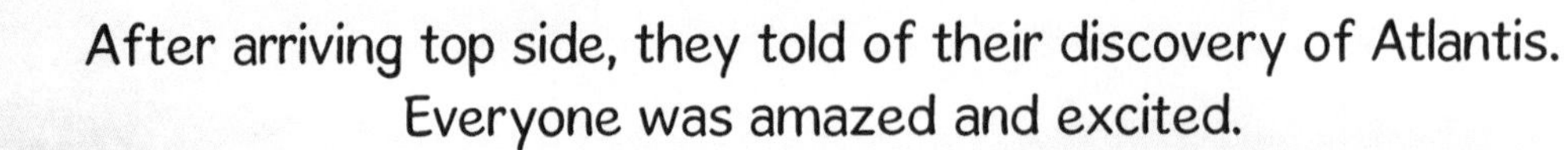

After arriving top side, they told of their discovery of Atlantis. Everyone was amazed and excited.

The next couple of days were a blur of activity. Teams of archeologists were flown to Antarctica. Buildings were set up, and everything was photographed. One group read the ancient writing around the city. Another group studied the buildings, pottery, and statues. There was a lot to be learned!

Alex and Victoria sat nearby, watching the activity and drinking hot chocolate. Petting Elmo at his feet, Alex smiled and said, "What an awesome adventure!"

Alex's mom smiled and said, "The End." That was the story of *Adventure in Antarctica*. His mother leaned over, kissed Alex lightly on the cheek, and said, "Until tomorrow night and your next adventure." She winked and said, "Sleep tight."

The End

Did You Know? Fact or Fiction

Antarctica: Is a polar region located at the earth's South Pole, opposite the arctic region.

Primary Language: Antarctic has no official language due to an Antarctic treaty. English, French, German, Maori, Norwegian, Ognian, Russian, and Swedish are the most popular languages spoken on the continent.

Regional Animals: Whales: (Orca, Humpback, Southern Right, Sperm and Fin) **Seals:** (Southern Elephant, Ross, Crabeaters, Leopard) **Penguins:** (Adelie, Emperor, Chinstrap and Gentoo) **Albatrosses**

Aurora: A natural light display in the sky particularly located in the Polar Regions. It is a collision of energetic charged particles with atoms in the high altitude atmosphere.

Atlantis: Is a mythical island that was said to have sunk into the ocean in a single night. The legend speaks of their people being the first to have great knowledge, language, and engineering. They were even thought to have travelled the oceans long before anyone else. Some think they were the first civilization while others say they were an alien colony.

DON'T MISS A SINGLE ADVENTURE

collect all of the Alexander books at
www.abedtimeadventure.com

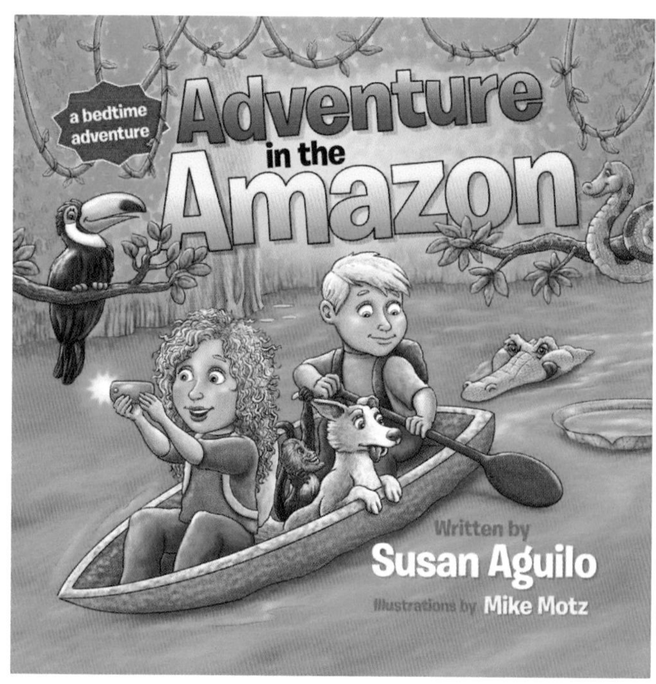

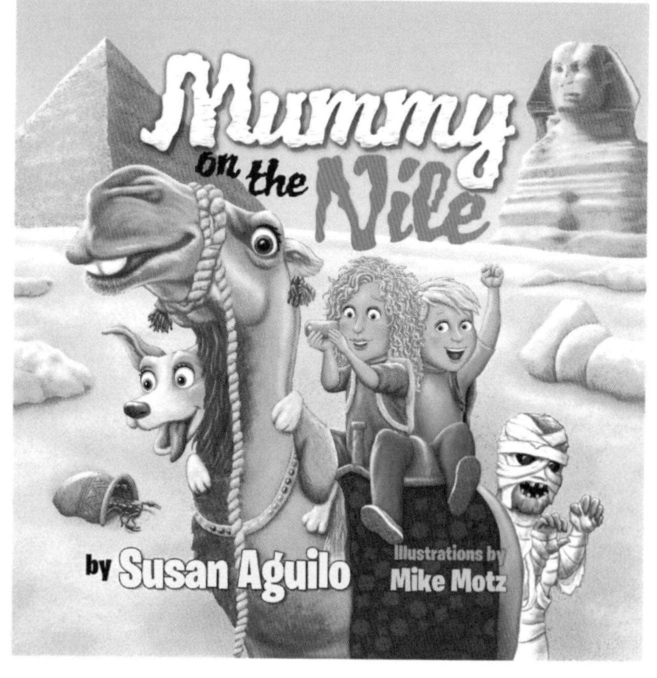

COMING SOON

www.abedtimeadventure.com

78697259R00024

Made in the USA
Columbia, SC
13 October 2017